Under Construction

By

Nick Kisella

First Printing

A Weber Pictures Publication

Cover Art By Ryan Scott Weber

Nick Kisella's photo by Stan Stronski

Kim, my love and best friend.
Nicholas Richard and Kimberly
Gayle, our twin babies.

Here's another one Rich-
Thanks Ryan

It Begins

The cop was young, not even thirty. He'd never pulled his gun out in the five years that he'd been on the force. He never wanted to be forced to, but he ended up pulling it out early that September morning.

He'd just picked up his morning coffee when he saw them, a man and a woman. They were both wearing white lab coats over business clothes. It looked like they were hugging. At least it did until he saw the blood.

There was a lot of blood.

"Freeze!" He shouted, running toward them. "Let go of him!" He yanked the woman's shoulder to pull her off and jumped back when she lunged at him.

The man, his throat and shoulder torn open and a bloody mess, fell to the ground in a heap. He just moaned and clutched at the wounds.

The cop fired his gun for the first time. He hit the woman right in the chest. The impact of the bullet sent her back a pace, but had no other effect on her. She kept coming at him.

"Lady, stop or I'll shoot again!" He shouted, holding his free hand out at her and backing up more.

Before he could get another shot off she was on him. She grabbed the arm he held out and growling, sunk her teeth into his forearm.

The cop screamed in agony and fired his gun again, inadvertently shooting her in the head. The woman fell to the ground and didn't move.

"Damn it!" He cradled his wounded arm. "I didn't mean to shoot her in the head!" He turned to the man that was on the ground, only he wasn't on the ground anymore.

He was on his feet, growling.

He lunged at the cop.

ONE

It was dark in the basement room.

There were no windows.

Nothing but a folding chair and an old metal cot.

Samantha was lying on the cot. It smelled musty and she cringed every time she thought of other people being in the same room, lying on the same cot. Maybe even dying on it.

The shackle around her wrist was loose enough for her to spin around. The chain hooked to the wall rattled every time she did it. It was long enough for her to walk from the cot to the chair, but no further.

The door was open. George left it that way for a few hours a night so she could get some fresh air, but it didn't matter, she couldn't get out.

She swore she'd heard sirens blaring somewhere outside from in the darkness. There was a lot noise coming from upstairs too, which she thought was weird because George lived alone.

George Daniels kidnapped Samantha Crane while she was at the Laundromat washing some heavy blankets she'd used at the beach.

It was late, and the Laundromat was empty. Sam, as her friends called her, thought it was the perfect time to get the blankets, which were too big for her own washer, cleaned. Summer was ending and she knew there wouldn't be time for another trip to the shore. Her job at Rainbow

Daycare always got too hectic at the end of the summer for her to take any vacation days.

Samantha was an inch over five feet tall. She had long, thick, auburn hair and dark brown, very expressive eyes. Her face was a soft oval, with full pouty lips skin like polished white marble. She never wore much make-up because she didn't like the way it felt on her skin and she was lucky enough to not need it.

That night she tied back her hair and threw on some sweats to cover her curvy shape; since there were usually a lot of single guys coming in and out of the Laundromat at night and she was in no mood to deal with any of them. “Single and loving it”, she said to herself. A pair of sneakers completed the picture; and she was off.

George came up behind her. She didn’t even know he was there at first, at least not until she felt the needle pinch her throat. After that the world was a spinning mess, and she found out her neighbor, whom she used to refer to as a nice middle-aged guy, was actually a serial killer.

"I usually get them from out of state, but I just couldn't take watching you anymore, seeing you living next to me, looking so much like 'Her'. I'll probably have to move after I'm finished with you, but I'm sure it'll be worth it." He smiled at her, and it was a smile she'll never forget because it was evil. Just evil, pure and simple.

She was handcuffed to the cot at the time, still feeling the effects of whatever he'd pumped into her system.

That was when he told her about some of the others; always redheads, short, and thirtyish.

He took out an old cigar box and showed her an assortment of rings and earrings that belonged to the women.

"You can borrow something to wear from here if you want to," he said with another evil grin. "I like them when they wear jewelry. Earrings are great, especially hoops;

gives me something to bite on while I'm doing my business."

Still groggy, Sam gagged, because she knew exactly what his 'business' was.

"Sometimes I just rip them off and throw 'em in the box." He flipped the lid closed and put the box aside.

"You're gonna be here for a while, so get used to the accommodations. I like it when they hang out in the 'quiet room' for a while before I spend time with them. If you want to scream go right ahead, no one will hear you. The 'quiet room' is just that; soundproof."

He tapped the walls.

Sam struggled against the handcuffs, but it was useless. She could barely move.

She couldn't tell how long she'd been there, but guessed at around three days because of the number of meals he brought her.

It had been a day since she pulled the tiny metal bracket off of the folding chair. She noticed it was loose when she sat down. That night she bent it back and forth until it snapped off.

In the meantime she acted very politely to George, because she was carefully grinding away at the cement around the hook in the wall where her chain was attached to. She wanted to keep him happy so she could stay alive long enough to get free.

The sirens got louder.

She took that as a cue to try to dig out some more of the hook. The metal made a slight scraping noise against the cement, which she hoped would be drowned out by all the sirens from outside.

She'd been careful to sweep the cement dust around so George wouldn't notice.

Sam was pulling on the hook while grinding away, and it had begun to come loose. Her heart was racing as more of the metal pulled free of the wall.

"C'mon," she whispered anxiously, digging around the hook even more determined than before.

Suddenly there was a crashing sound upstairs, and she heard glass shatter.

More digging; grinding the metal from the chair into the cements. Sam had no idea what was going on upstairs, she just wanted out.

A small bit of cement cracked and fell to the floor and the hook moved. It was nearly out.

Just then she could hear George fling open the basement door and come running down the stairs.

He was shouting but she couldn't understand what he was saying. There was the sound of more footfalls behind him as if he were being followed.

A light came on. Sam winced at its sudden brightness, but continued to grind away the cement, sweat forming on her forehead as anxiety took hold.

"Get away from me!" Sam heard George shout as he got closer to the 'quiet room'.

She pulled the hook out of the wall. A huge sense of relief filled her and she jerked herself upright and began to reel in the chain.

George ran past the door.

There was a shuffling sound coming from the other side of the basement, from where George had come from. Sam didn't wait around to see who it was. She made a dash for the door, saw George unlocking a Bilco door leading outside and ran up behind him.

She freed up a length of chain that was a couple of feet long and flung it over George's head so it smacked him in the throat. Then she pulled it tight, holding her shoulder against his back.

"Open that door and let me the fuck out of here or I'll kill you, I swear I'll kill you!" She shouted.

George coughed loudly, grabbing the chain and trying to pull it away from his throat.

"You idiot!" he said with a gurgle. "They're coming, let go of me so I can open the door."

Samantha yanked him up and shouted in his ear. "Give me the fuckin' key to this goddamn shackle or I swear I'll snap your neck right now!"

George flung his hand up, the key ring swinging from one of his fingers. Sam held the chain tight with one of her hands and grabbed the keys with the other.

She let the chain loosen a bit so he could continue opening the door and unlocked the shackle that had already drawn blood on her wrist. He started to pull the open lock out of the latch on the door when she heard the shuffling getting closer behind them and turned to see who was there.

Her eyes bulged when she saw three people shuffling toward them. They were bloody and moaning, dragging their feet as if their ankles were broken. One of them was missing part of his cheek, teeth on that side of his face exposed in a gruesome display.

"Who the fuck are they?" She shouted, pulling the chain tighter. "

George said nothing; he just gasped and kicked up on the door leading outside. It flung open and then Samantha saw the night sky for the first time in days.

She thought she'd never see it again after getting locked up.

TWO

The neighborhood was called 'Clinton Heights'. It was an upscale neighborhood and there were only about a dozen homes in it. Each was very large with at least an acre of property around them. It wasn't a gated community, the residents wanted to keep it simple for the time being.

Tony had a job at the largest house in the neighborhood.

It was a huge house. So immense that Tony jokingly referred to it as 'The Taj', short for Taj Mahal. He'd never worked on such a large elaborately decorated house before.

"Seriously, how big do you think this place really is?" Richie said, grabbing the paint rollers from the back of Tony's truck. He was in his early twenties and wore a gray t-shirt with 'Armed and Dangerous' emblazoned on the front of it. The back had the same lettering and a bunch of different tools under it.

“It’s got to be at least fifteen-thousand square feet.” Tony said, sipping on his morning coffee. He tipped back the baseball hat he always wore and started to get his game plan for the day together in his head.

Tony Marelli owned ‘Armed and Dangerous’. It was a small construction company he’d started a few years prior that generally did repairs and construction for high-end houses. He had three employees, and usually they didn’t work on the same job, but ‘The Taj’ was huge, and the quicker the job was finished, the more money it would net, so he had all three men meet him there at the crack of dawn.

Angelina, the owner of 'The Taj' had used his company frequently for everything from putting up a chandelier to changing light switches. It was a pain fitting her into the schedule sometimes if the job was really small or frivolous, but he always got around to her.

"What is it this time?" Mike smirked. "Does she have mirrors or something for us to hang?"

"Well, it's an easy job but a hell of a lot bigger than hanging mirrors." He looked over at Richie, the youngest member of their crew. "You got those paint rollers?"

Richie pushed his glasses up and looked confused for a second then he realized he was already carrying them and nodded.

"Okay then, as soon as Joe gets here we can go in and get started." He sipped his coffee again and walked toward Mike. "She's got all the supplies we need already in the basement. There's a lot of painting to do which is why I needed you guys to get here so early. I figured if we get an early enough start we can bang it out in a day."

"So, we're painting the basement?" Mike asked. "But wasn't it just painted a month or so ago?"

"Yeah, but she didn't like the color anymore." Tony rolled his eyes and tossed his empty coffee cup into the back of his truck, suppressing a grin.

"Is she even home?" Richie asked, approaching them with an armload of paint rollers.

"No, she said she'd call me sometime this morning. Her and her family are on vacation. Their flight back is supposed to be this morning."

A silver jeep pulled up the long driveway. It turned sharply and parked between Mike's truck and Richie's Toyota.

Joe got out and nodded to them.

"Nice of you to show up." Mike said, joking because Joe was usually always the first man at a jobsite.

"Yeah, I thought it would be nice to work today." He commented with a smile. "What's on the agenda? It must be a big one with all of us here."

"The basement." Tony said, gesturing to Richie and the paint rollers. "We gotta paint it."

"But didn't we just-"

"Yep, we did," Mike made a face. "But Angelina doesn't like that color anymore."

"So we're gonna be here all day and probably tomorrow, too?" Joe asked, following the rest of the group up to the front door.

"Well, if we put in a good day and maybe work a little late we can bang it all out and be done with it." Tony said, pulling the house key out of the aluminum portfolio he had under his arm. He unlocked the door and then quickly hit a series of numbers into the alarm pad inside.

"We should be fine, she's always got a lot of food for us and her CD collection is great." Mike smiled, remembering how fun it was last time. They worked, sure, but the music and munchies made it feel fun, like they were just hanging out painting a friend's house.

The house was dark inside. Tony flicked on the lights and a huge chandelier hanging directly above them lit up brightly.

"I still wonder how they clean it." Richie said, looking annoyed. "All that crystal is a waste."

"Well, it's a waste they enjoy and can afford." Tony quirked an eyebrow up at him and headed to the basement door. It was a solid oak door behind an enormous staircase leading upstairs. There were four bedrooms upstairs, a master suite, and an extra living room. Tony couldn't remember exactly how many bathrooms there were, but there were at least three.

The basement consisted of four areas. There was a playroom for the children, which was a very large room with a television on one wall. The room next to it was a gym, with a Universal, free weights, and a treadmill. The next room was actually where they'd entered the basement, which was a 'Theater Room', where there were several large reclining couches situated around a large screen. A projector hung from the ceiling, and there was an old fashioned popcorn maker in the corner of the room.

Adjoined to that room was a spare bedroom with its own bathroom and living room. A huge kitchen and dining room came off of there where there were two wine cellars. One of them was refrigerated.

"It never ceases to amaze me, how big this basement is." Mike looked around and shook his head.

"The place is so big we could live here and no one would even know."

"True," Tony said pointing to the kitchen. "And there are no windows except for those." There was a window above the sink in the kitchen and another in the door leading outside. There was a staircase right outside the door that led up to the side driveways and the garage doors.

"Well boys, let's get started." Tony said.

THREE

The stars were so bright and the feeling of the cool air against her face brought such elation that she nearly forgot what her situation was.

Sam pulled back on the chain, hearing George gurgle and clutch at his throat as he fell backwards onto the cement floor.

"Get down and stay down you son of a bitch before I strangle you!"

Sam looked back to the people coming up on them and flung George toward them, releasing the chain.

She was still wearing her sweats from the night she was kidnapped, but George had taken her sneakers.

"I don't give a fuck if I'm barefoot!" Without another thought she dashed through the basement door and up the five steps into the darkness of the night.

When Sam got to the top of the stairs she was ready to run to her house and call the police, but the sight that met her eyes when she was out in the open forced her back into the shadows, shocked beyond reckoning.

Huddled down between a bush and the open Bilco door she nervously rubbed her sore blood-crusted wrist and stared in disbelief.

Her neighborhood, which she once considered too quiet, was suddenly a flurry of violent activity and thundering noise.

There were people running from all directions, bleeding and screaming in the streets. She could see a car on fire twisted around a tree with the driver still inside a few houses down.

Directly across the street from her there was a family desperately trying to escape, their car packed but surrounded by so many people that it wasn't going anywhere.

The sounds filling the air sent a chill up her spine. The screams, the snarling; it was as if she walking into a riot filled with people and wild animals.

There was a sound of glass shattering and numerous car alarms were going off at the same time.

It was total chaos.

"What the hell is going on?"

She mumbled fearfully, debating whether or not to make a break for her house and risk being seen.

FOUR

Four hours of painting and Richie's phone started to die. He hated the new phone he bought a few weeks ago because the battery never lasted long, but he loved the fact that he could do anything with it. He'd been going online all morning and even got some shopping done.

"Hey Tony I'm gonna go out to my car for a minute. I'll be right back." He said, leaving before he could hear any protesting from Tony.

He walked to the back of the basement and went out through the side door near the kitchen.

As tall as he was, he took the stairs two at a time and winced at the bright sunlight when it hit him in the face. It was barely dawn when they'd arrived.

"I hate this working at the 'crack of dawn' shit!" He declared adamantly.

There were no cars parked at the side of the house, they were all safely tucked away in the garages. He got to the front driveway and saw that the landscapers had arrived.

There were two lawnmowers sitting on the side of the road next to the dump truck and trailer that brought them there. They were running, idling slowly, but there was no one around.

"That's weird," he mumbled.

Richie looked all over on the way toward his car. All he saw were some paper coffee cups lying on the road, but none of the usual workers.

Richie didn't speak Spanish, but he always greeted the group of guys when they were there together working. He imagined being nice to them could very well come in handy someday if he ever needed a job in a pinch, or maybe even a gallon of gas if he was running too low to reach the nearest gas station.

He got to his little foreign car and snatched up his phone charger from the middle console between the front seats. He started to plug the phone into the charger when he felt something nudge him. Richie dropped his phone suddenly and shook his head, annoyed.

"What?" he said, pulling himself out of the car, thinking that he would see either Joe or Mike there ready to make some sort of sarcastic comment about him using his phone while on the job again.

What he saw was one of the landscapers. He was a little over five feet tall and stocky. Like the rest of the landscapers, he wore a baseball hat, shorts and a sweatshirt. It was like their informal uniform.

There was a bandage wrapped around his left calf. It was soaked with blood, and the leg itself looked a little on the gray-side.

"That's a nasty cut you've got there." Richie sounded concerned and a little grossed out. "Did you need something or what?" he asked, waiting for some sort of response.

The man, eyes downcast, lifted his head up and unexpectedly lunged for Richie.

Surprised and a bit confused, Richie pushed the man away, wincing when he inadvertently smelled the man's breath.

"Get the fuck away from me! What the hell is your problem?" Richie said angrily, pushing his glasses up.

The man stumbled back, then growled and paced forward toward him again.

The growling gave Richie a cold chill, and suddenly he wasn't shocked or confused; he was afraid.

"People don't growl." he thought to himself. He pushed the man back again, hard enough to knock him down, and turned away, running back to the house.

He didn't care that at the time he'd left both his phone and the charger for it in the car.

FIVE

Samantha heard George struggling below fighting off whoever was down there. The struggling turned into George screaming. Sam was just glad that he couldn't follow her, and part of her wished she could see what was happening to him, but then she was suddenly concerned with being seen because of the noise.

She still didn't understand what happened, but whoever was attacking George had allowed her to find freedom just by being there, and she wasn't about to give it up.

Heart racing, she ducked low and ran across the lawn to her house next door; hugging any shadows she could cling to in order to avoid being seen by anyone in the surrounding area. Sam couldn't bear the thought of being confronted by anyone, still more than shaken by George kidnapping her.

The backyard was quiet. She crept around the house and grabbed the spare key she had hidden in an artificial rock under a bush and let herself in the backdoor as quietly as she could.

Sam locked the door behind her and put the chain on it. She didn't turn the lights on she just ran to the phone to call the police and promptly found out that the phone wasn't working.

"What the fuck is going on! This is crazy!" She said, eyes filling with tears. She took the phone with her to the living room where she was able to peek out the curtains of the front window.

The street in front of her house was turning into a battlefield of people and cars and she had no idea why.

"Maybe there's something on the news." Her words were desperate sounding as she fished for a remote, but she didn't let herself cry.

Cable was out.

She flicked off the television, angrily threw the remote on the nearby couch and stood there hugging herself.

Samantha had gone from one life and death situation to another and at the moment all she wanted to do was scream and cry. Her legs were shaking and her hands trembled.

"I've got to keep it together," her whisper sounded determined and her hands clenched into fists.

She thought about getting into her garage to try to escape it all in her car, but then realized that her car was still at the Laundromat several blocks away, or had more than likely been towed away, impounded by then for being parked there so long. The curses she uttered did nothing to dissipate her anger.

“That sick son of a bitch took my purse too.” She squeezed her eyes shut, trying to suppress a sob when she thought of how her keys, wallet and cell phone were in her purse.

She considered going back to the house to retrieve her belongings, but knew she couldn’t chance it. Sam couldn’t risk staying in her own house either with all the insanity going on outside.

"Yeah, I'm safe for the moment, but if someone tries to break in I'm screwed." She thought to herself. "It's just a matter of time."

Sam remembered that she had a mountain bike in the garage. It had been collecting dust for at least a year, but she knew the tires were still filled with air because she saw it every day when she got in her car to go to work.

"It's not much but it'll have to do for now." She assured herself.

An only child, Samantha had lost her parents, one after the other, to cancer two years prior.

She couldn't have felt more alone had she planned things herself. The few friends she had were close, but there was no way to get in touch with any of them with no phone or car. The only escape she knew of was a small cabin that her parents had in Pennsylvania. She'd inherited it but hadn't visited there since her parents had died. It was a long shot, but the only one she could think of at the moment.

It was off the beaten path, but that's what she wanted at the moment. The only issue was getting there. She was in the middle of New Jersey, while the cabin was a two hour drive away.

"Maybe I can ride the bike until I can get my hands on a car somewhere." She surmised, then couldn't help but laugh at her own words. "Listen to me, 'gangsta car thief'. Not!"

With a plan in mind, she felt a little better, a little stronger.

Sam made sure the front door was locked with the chain on it. She pushed a heavy table in front of it and grabbed a dining room chair to prop under the doorknob. She grabbed a flashlight that she kept in the kitchen for emergencies and did the same to the backdoor, keeping the light low.

From there Samantha raced upstairs trying not to think about what would happen if anyone broke in through the windows. She wanted to grab a kitchen knife but favored the baseball bat she had from her softball playing days upstairs if she needed a weapon.

There was an old backpack that she used when hiking was somewhat of a hobby years ago while she was in college. It was at the back of her bedroom closet with the bat. She grabbed them, some fresh sweats, underwear, socks and an older pair of sneakers before running into the bathroom.

She felt filthy. The days she was held captive seemed like forever and she smelled so bad it disgusted her enough to risk taking a few minutes to shower quickly.

Sam had to literally peel her sweatshirt off, and her bra, which always strained against her size 44D chest, had torn just below the straps. She didn't realize how much wearing it had hurt until she took it off.

After she slid down her sweatpants and thong she caught an image of herself in the full length mirror on the back of the bathroom door and sighed sadly.

She was a mess.

Sam's hair was a knotted mass of auburn curls, and her skin was pale. Her eyes were sunken in and had dark circles around them. Standing there naked she nearly laughed upon the realization that she looked like a strung-out busty porn star.

With the flashlight on the counter, pointing to the open shower, Sam bathed, soaping up quickly, the bat leaning next to the shower always in sight and her ears straining for any sound other than that of the water.

When she was done she dried off hastily and dressed. It was difficult to get a brush through her hair but not as bad as she expected. She simply tied her damp hair back into a ponytail, and packed her toothbrush and other personal items in the backpack.

The fridge was her next stop. The milk was spoiled, but Sam was more interested and grabbing the bottled water she had there. The pantry didn't have much but she was able to grab a few things like crackers, hash and even a can of spam. There were some apples in the fruit bowl on the kitchen table still fresh enough to take. She dumped them in the backpack and tied it shut after adding a box of matches, an old radio and all the batteries she could find.

The garage was dark, but Sam could see the first light of day coming through the windows of the automatic garage door.

She checked the window in the backdoor. When she was satisfied that there wasn't anyone roaming around in the backyard, she cleared and unlocked the door.

Easing the bike through the door was difficult to do quietly, but she managed well enough. Swinging the backpack over her shoulders, she mounted the bike and rode off across the back lawn. For the time being she decided to stick to the backyards and avoid any people she saw for as long as possible.

SIX

Richie nearly tripped up when he jumped down the stairs. He got back in the basement of 'The Taj', slammed and locked the door, clearly out of breath.

"What the hell are you doing Richie?" Tony said. He put down the paint roller he was using on the far wall and approached him with a quizzical expression. "Why are you locking the door?"

Tony could hear his phone ring from across the room. He dismissed the 'Peter Gunn' theme, figuring it was either his wife, mother, or Angelina. Any of the three could wait a minute while he found out why Richie was acting so whacky.

"You're never gonna believe me!" Richie said in a rush. Then he slammed the palm of his hand into his forehead. "Damn it! I left my phone and the charger out there!"

Mike and Joe heard Richie from the 'Theater Room'.

"Sounds like Richie is having a bit of a problem." Joe grinned.

"So what else is new?" Mike said sarcastically. "The kids got more issues than a magazine rack. Let's go see what's happening."

Mike put his brush down and stepped down from the ladder where he was cutting in.

"Why not? I can use a break anyway." Joe finished the spot he was painting then put the roller down. "Why don't we see what

Angelina left us to eat while we're at it? It's a good time for a break anyway."

They got to the kitchen area and saw Tony with his hand on Richie's back, trying to calm him down.

"What's goin' on?" Joe asked Tony, unexpectedly concerned when he saw them. "Did something happen to him?"

"Richie says one of the landscapers attacked him out there," Tony shook his head looking confused. He went over to the kitchen counter where he left his phone and saw that he had a voicemail.

"You're kidding, right?" Mike sounded slightly annoyed as he pulled a bottle of water out of the fridge.

"He was fuckin' growling at me like an animal!" Richie spouted angrily. "You should have seen him! He looked crazy!"

"Don't get me wrong, but aren't those guys all like, 'munchkin' size?" Joe said. Mike could barely keep a straight face.

"Hold on guys, I can't hear." Tony said, holding his phone up to his ear. "I got a voicemail from Angelina."

The voicemail sounded very garbled, Tony could barely understand what she was saying.

"Our flight home has been delayed. We're all stuck here on the plane. They're telling us that there's been some sort of viral outbreak and we're going to have to wait for the CDC to come in and examine everyone for symptoms. We've been on this plane since yesterday if you

factor in the change in time. I never heard anything about any virus before we left. I guess you can just finish up and bill me. I'll call you when I find anything else out or if we can get off the plane."

"Wow." Tony shook his head. "Angelina and her family are stuck on her flight back. They won't let it off the ground, something about a virus. Did you guys hear anything about it?"

The three of them shook their heads.

"I didn't even bother listening to the news this morning since I had to be out the door so quick." Mike said.

"I never heard anything either," Tony said. "Maybe it's just going on where she's flying from, I don't know which airport she called from. Let's just finish up here as soon as we can. It's going to be a long day."

"What about Richie?" Joe asked. "What do we do about the 'munchkins' outside?"

"Stop fuckin' talkin' about me like I'm not here! And they're not 'munchkins'!" Richie snapped angrily.

"You really expect us to believe one of them attached you?" Joe grinned. "They can't even speak English."

"That's really not the point guys." Tony shook his head. "We're all here to work, and it should really be a safe environment for everyone while we're here." He turned to face Mike and Joe. "None of us know what happened out there. We weren't with Richie when he went outside. For all we know it could have been even worse than the way he described it."

"Then let's get out there and see what the hell is going on." Mike said. He looked at Richie. "You gotta get your phone and charger anyway, right?"

Richie nodded, but still looked nervous. He had a bad feeling about the entire situation, but followed the three of them outside anyway.

SEVEN

Samantha took a break shortly after dawn, stopping at an empty scenic overlook near Martinsville. She leaned her bike against a thick old oak tree and slowly sat down. Her legs and butt were incredibly sore. Sitting, it was as if she felt each individual muscle of her lower body; and they weren't happy.

She was exhausted. There was nothing else to call it. Still, it surprised her that she was able to get as far as she did without collapsing. She'd hoped to have found a car somewhere by then but after seeing what was going on all around her Sam felt lucky to have avoided it and just be alive.

The bike allowed her a lot of maneuverability, but she had to work on her speed, her legs hurt so much that after a while they were just numb. She had her doubts being able to escape at first, though she wouldn't allow herself to dwell on them.

Riding the bike through the neighborhood wasn't too difficult. She had to bypass a few fences but that wasn't really too difficult. It gave her a glimpse of the chaos on the streets. She blocked out the screaming and gunfire and pedaled nonstop.

At one point she was nearly hit by a car driving onto a front lawn while trying to go around a fence. The car was in flames and there were people clinging to it howling.

Sam pushed on, forcing herself not to look past a first glance.

"Just pedal," she thought to herself. "Pedal until you can't anymore!"

The worst of the trouble began after she rode outside the confines of her neighborhood, beyond the somewhat closed off residential area that had been her home for years.

The streets were crowded with beeping cars and pedestrians. Some people were running, others trudging along in a daze; or at least that's what she thought at the time.

There was a lot of blood.

People tried to grab her.

They were throwing things, trying to knock her off the bike. Some of them snarled at her, snapping their jaws as if they were trying to bite her.

Gunshots, she heard them all around her and felt a bullet whiz by her chest while trying to find an alternate route around a grocery store.

The store had been wrecked. The windows were shattered and

from what she saw passing by people were still looting it.

Her white-knuckled grip on the handlebars was the only thing preventing her from trembling in fear. Her legs pumped and though her lungs burned like a blast furnace she sped away.

Police were all over but didn't seem to be doing a whole lot to help anyone. She watched a few officers getting attacked while a block away others were shooting what looked to be innocent people trying to escape the insanity.

The radio. It was old, and worked as a police scanner as well using a nine-volt battery. It was digital, so it was modern enough to pick up stations and the local police from the surrounding area, but much too large and cumbersome in comparison to anything that had come out in the past five years.

Sam tried to listen in on the police band at first to see if she could find out about any real trouble spots nearby in order to avoid them, but the sound was so jumbled and filled with static that she ended up settling on listening to a local FM station.

There was no music, just people talking about the gridlocked highways, and then the news abruptly cut in.

"- still haven't found the origin of the virus. Terrorism hasn't been ruled out and there's still a question as to whether it's terrestrial or extraterrestrial, having arrived on a fallen piece of space debris or in some other such manner."

The woman's voice was calm and resolute, but there was an

occasional edge to it, as if she were about to break down. Needless to say, she paused occasionally and when she did there was dead air.

"All I can truly report right now is that because of all the street violence and looting the President has instated Marshall Law as of this morning, and the military has been brought in to help police departments nationwide regain control of things ."

"All flights in and out of the United States have been canceled with passengers being detained and

screened for the virus before being allowed off their planes."

"Citizens are to stay where they are or find a reasonable safe place to fall back in until more government facilities are provided for them. Lock windows and doors, or stay in basements."

"The virus has only been on record and active for the past thirty-six hours. During the past twenty-four hours the viral outbreak has grown exponentially, with hospitals being overrun with the infected and wounded. The dead have been rising

and filling our streets and infecting even more people."

She paused for a long moment, and Sam could have sworn she heard her sob in the background.

"I did not misquote, it has recently been reported by the CDC that the virus has affected the recently deceased, reanimating corpses. These animated bodies are very functionally limited, but seemingly impervious to pain and injury. They continue to show signs of motor skills after being shot or even when limbs have been severed. With no capacity

for reason, they have been seen roaming the streets, showing cannibalistic tendencies."

"Government researchers are analyzing specimens in an attempt to find a cure or at least a way to stop these infected walking corpses, or 'zombies', a word that has reluctantly been used to describe them of late."

The rest of the newscast was a blur of noise to Samantha. Her mind was stuck on the word 'zombie' and the idea of the recently deceased coming back to life.

"They were really trying to bite me, eat me, and I didn't even know it!" She cringed, grossed out and terrified at the same time.

Now that Sam knew the truth of what was going on she almost wished George had killed her while she was captive in his basement.

The dead are being reanimated.

"I was shackled in the basement of a killer when it all happened." She thought to herself, trembling. "I missed the outbreak but now I'm stuck in it!"

Sam realized that George's house must have been invaded by those creatures, and he must have run down to the basement to escape them through the back door, only to be handed over by her on a silver platter so she could get away.

"I killed him." Sam said flatly when she thought of how she tossed him aside to the three 'people' in his basement. "I might just as well have killed him myself."

She couldn't believe it bothered her so much, but then Sam realized that there hasn't been any time for her to really stop and process everything that's happened to her since George kidnapped her. Her mind had been in panic mode ever since she was abducted.

The news had enlightened her to more than she wanted to know and she had to deal with it.

The cabin was still her destination, but she needed a vehicle, something strong and safe to drive. Sam could remember the area relatively well. There were some very large houses around her, and most of them had more than one garage.

"If I can find an area, maybe a block or at least a few houses grouped together, where there aren't too many of these things maybe I can break in and get some wheels." She thought to herself. "May I can even get some more supplies."

Agonizingly, she stood up and stretched, feeling every ache and pain. Ignoring it all, Sam grabbed the bike and flipped her leg over it. Beginning to pedal again, slowly, building up speed, she rode out of the scenic overlook praying all the way.

EIGHT

"There's nobody here." Joe shook his head and stepped over to the lawnmowers. They weren't running as Richie had said they were. He tried to touch the engines but they were too hot.

"They must have run out of gas." Tony said, looking around warily. "This doesn't make sense. The neighborhood is usually quiet but the landscapers should be somewhere."

"Well, I don't know what his name was but he looked all kinds of fucked up!" Richie walked back to his car.

"I don't hear anyone else on the block doing their lawn either." Mike approached them. "I checked around by our trucks. There's no one there either. Maybe they're helping one of the neighbors with something?"

"For this long?" Tony sounded skeptical. "No, something's gotta be up. I'm gonna go check their truck."

"I'll come with you." Mike followed him.

As Richie got to his car he didn't notice that the door had been closed since he gone back to the house. He didn't even think about it as he reached out to open it and retrieve his phone and charger.

"Joe how long do you think the lawnmowers were running? It had to have been a few hours, right?" He turned his head to where Joe was, not paying attention to his car as he pulled open the door.

The landscaper was lying down inside his car. He sat up and lunged for Richie's arm.

Joe's eyes widened when he saw the man inside Richie's car go after his arm.

"Richie! Look out!" Joe jumped up and started to run toward him.

"What?" He turned to look at his car just as the man inside grabbed his arm and snarling, sunk his teeth into his bare forearm.

Richie screamed.

Joe got there a second later and kicked the man off of Richie, pulling him away from the car. Richie shrieked and grabbed his arm with his hand, holding the wound as blood gushed.

"Shit man! What the fuck?" Richie shouted, suddenly weak in the knees at the sight of his own blood. He nearly fell, and if it wasn't for Joe half-carrying him back toward the house, he would have.

"Oh Christ!" Tony shouted, when he and Mike heard Richie scream.

When they saw what was happening to him they ran back

there right before they would have reached the landscapers' truck.

"Mike call 911!" Tony shouted back at him.

Mike pulled his phone out while trying to keep up. He hit the numbers but there was no service.

"It's not working Tony!" He shoved it back in his pocket. "There's no service!"

They didn't see the door of the truck flip open behind them, or see the bloody man struggle and then fall out of it. He moaned and leaning against the truck for balance, pushed himself up to his feet, shuffling with surprising speed toward Mike and Tony.

"Guys! Behind you!" Joe called out, still dragging Richie along, when he saw the man coming up behind Mike and Tony.

Mike, who was still a few steps behind Tony, turned and saw the guy coming at them. He gagged, but held down his breakfast, smacking Tony in the back.

"How the fuck is this guy still standing! He can't be alive!" He shouted to his boss, pointing behind him.

The man coming at them was missing large sections of flesh on his right arm. The limb was just hanging there with blood covering it. His face was initially what affected Mike the most.

The entire right side of the man's face was covered in blood, and the area where his eye should been have been was torn away. There was no eye, no cheek, just bloody visible bone and shredded muscle.

"Holy shit!" Tony said. He looked at Mike with bulging eyes, sweat suddenly forming on his brow. 'This can't be real! Somebody has to be playing some kind of a joke on us!" Tony insisted.

"I don't know Tony he doesn't look too fake to me." Mike said warily.

Just then from the side of the house another landscaper appeared. He was carrying hedge trimmers. The sweatshirt he wore was matted with blood and his throat was torn open. The man seemed to be able to walk with more stability in comparison to the other two, going right after Joe and Richie.

"Tony we gotta do something!" Mike said. "We gotta stop them!"

"Weapons!" Tony grabbed Mike's arm and pulled him along. "We gotta get to the truck. Hammers, crowbars, anything we can swing at them!"

NINE

Samantha saw cars less and less the further she drove. There were no people either, alive or dead, roaming the streets.

"This is really weird." She mumbled. "Where is everybody?"

She was traveling through a residential area and guessed that the majority of the people that lived there were already on the road or locked up in their houses trying to wait things out.

She started to ride up an exceptionally steep hill when she thought she heard a lawn mower running.

"Who the hell would be cutting their grass at a time like this?" She said aloud, turning to follow the noise. She thought about it for a minute then declared, "Maybe they have a truck and wouldn't mind a passenger!"

Sam turned the bike toward where she heard the sound and

pedaled as hard as she could in that direction.

Rounding a turn she spotted a landscaping truck with a trailer parked in front of what must have been the largest house she'd ever seen.

There were real people there, and from the distance she thought she saw them getting attacked by what looked like three dead landscapers.

The bike skidded to a halt and she jumped off, pulling free her baseball bat, running toward the scene.

Tony had two buckets of tools in the back of his truck along with several other power tools. He jumped into the bed of the truck and tossed a hammer to Mike. He took a crowbar for himself and jumped back down.

"Let's take these bastards down!" He shouted, racing toward the man that was closing in on Joe and Richie.

The man looked dead. Tony had decided in his head that the man really was dead but somehow still walking. "That's got to be it," he thought adamantly. "Somehow these dead guys are still on their feet!"

He swung the crowbar at the man, smacking his arms and knocking the hedge trimmers away. The trimmers hit the ground and the man didn't even notice, he just continued on, trying to grab at Tony.

Without a word Tony slammed the crowbar into the man's chest, knocking him backward. He stood over him, and before he could rise to his feet Tony smashed him in the head and chest repeatedly.

At the same time Mike went after the man that bit Richie. He swung the hammer low and fast, hitting him in the left knee. The man went down with a snort, and then began pulling himself across the ground and grabbing for Mike.

"You ain't gettin' me you bastard!" Mike shouted. He smashed him in the arm then hit him in the chest and worked his way up until he smashed his skull.

Mike went down to his knees, swinging the hammer, battering him until his arm was too tired to swing the hammer anymore.

He turned just in time to see the one-eyed man approach him from behind. He struggled to get to his feet when he heard a thumping sound, as if a melon had been smashed on the ground.

The one-eyed man abruptly fell to the ground directly in front of him with a dull thud, not moving again.

Standing there behind the body was a short auburn haired woman dressed in sweats. She was panting and tightly grasping a bloody baseball bat.

"I got him!" Sam shouted. "I really got him!"

Mike got to his feet and held out his hands, palms out, at the woman standing in front of him holding a baseball bat.

"Hey, everything's fine now." He said nervously. "I'm normal! Don't hit me! I'm okay!"

"No, no I wouldn't hit you!" She said taking a deep breath. "I just wanted to stop that dead guy before he could try to eat you."

It didn't dawn on Sam how strange what she said sounded until the words were out there.

"We have to get inside." Tony said running up to them. "It looks like all the noise we made has attracted a few more." He pointed to where two more slow moving people were walking up the street toward them. They looked very much like the men they had just beaten down.

"Who are you?" Tony asked Sam as she followed them back to the house.

"My name's Samantha." She said following Tony and Mike down the stairs and into the basement. "Call me Sam."

"She saved my ass out there." Mike commented, slamming and locking the door behind them.

Joe had already gotten Richie down there, leaving a trail of blood. He had Richie at the sink, running hot water over the bite he'd received, trying to clean it up using a fresh rag from their painting supplies.

"Do we have anything we can use as a bandage?" Joe called out. "Something long enough to wrap around his arm?"

Tony went into the bathroom and grabbed a towel. He pulled out his razor knife, cut it into two long strips and brought them to Joe.

"Here, that'll have to do for now." Tony looked at Joe nervously. "How bad does it look?"

"I'm sure as hell no doctor, but I can tell you right now it's a really bad bite, tore some skin right off." Joe responded, worried looking. "It's really deep." He shook his. "I think that son of a bitch might have hit bone."

Richie was sweating bullets and wincing in pain.

"They've gotta have some kind of painkillers in the house somewhere!" He shouted to Joe. "Please, it burns! My whole arm! Try to get me something for the pain! Anything!"

Samantha stood there staring sadly at Richie.

"He's infected." She whispered.

"What?" Mike asked, overhearing her. "Infected?"

"It's the virus." She said quietly. "He has it now."

"Virus?" Tony asked, trying 911 on his phone to no avail. "Damn it how can there not be any service!" He looked up at Sam. "What virus? What do you know about this?"

"I heard about it from the radio." Sam said nervously. "Those people out there are dead. They must have been infected somehow."

Joe's eyes widened. He looked at Richie and shook his head again.

"Tony can we get him something for pain?" He looked around the kitchen. "Anything, even some booze? I can probably clean this out better too if we had something."

"Sure." He went over to the bar next to the refrigerated wine cellar and grabbed the first bottle of whiskey he saw.

Joe took the bottle and poured some whiskey on the wound. Richie tensed up and screamed. He would have collapsed had Mike not been there to grab him.

"Drink some of this, it'll help." Joe said pushing the bottle at Richie. He chugged some, coughed violently, then chugged some more.

Joe wrapped the wound tight with the strips of towel that Tony gave him and then he and Tony helped him over to the spare bedroom.

"Keep drinking this." Tony said, putting the bottle in Richie's good hand. "It'll help a little until we can get an ambulance here."

Mike kept trying his phone and even the internet, but there was nothing.

"How is it that nothing's working?" He said irritated. "This doesn't make any sense! We should just get him to one of our trucks and drive to the hospital!"

"It's not safe to drive." Sam said. "The hospitals are full anyway."

"What the hell are you talking about? Where did you hear all this shit from?" Tony said angrily.

"Is there a radio or television that works here?" Sam asked. "The cable was out by me, but I heard a newscast on the radio. It explained everything to me." She dropped her backpack, pulling out the radio. Before she could turn it on Tony put his hand on her shoulder and gestured toward the playroom.

"C'mon, there's a TV in the kids playroom, maybe it works." Tony said rushing there with her and Mike close behind.

Joe got there after making sure Richie was covered up in bed. They all stood in front of the TV when Tony turned it on. There was nothing but snow on the first few channels he hit, and then there was a beeping sound and a black screen on a few. Nothing else.

"Okay." Tony said, trying to keep it together. "Why don't we just leave that on for the time being. Just in case there's an emergency broadcast later in the day."

Mike nodded. "The stations might just be working with a skeleton crew because of what's going. I mean, who would want to be there at work instead of home with their families when something like this is going on?"

"Yeah," Tony said with a sigh. "Do you still have that radio? Does it work?" He looked at Samantha hopefully.

"Yeah, I'll go get it." She said, rushing out to get it.

"Maybe we should stay in here, so Richie doesn't hear it." Joe suggested.

"Yeah, good idea." Mike agreed.

Sam returned with the radio and put it on top of an end table next to a small couch. They all stood around staring at it as she turned it on and tuned in the station she'd listened to earlier in the day.

What she heard on the road was being rebroadcasted.

"It's a recording of what I already heard." She said, clearly disappointed.

The guys listened to it intently, eyes narrow and shaking their heads. The broadcast ended with a live commentator coming on to add the latest information.

He had a tired sounding voice.

"We're still running here at WTOK but we're down to two people now, so this may be out final live broadcast for today. We're considering one live broadcast at noon each day, so check with us tomorrow."

"In the meantime, I'm afraid there isn't much to add to what's already been said. We do currently know of an effective method to stop the infected dead. Because the virus affects the sections of the brain that

control basic instinct and motor functions a blow to the head can disable or completely stop them. They seem to be concentrated in highly populated areas like industrial parks, malls, any densely populated city. If you're still alive, not infected, and in one of those areas get out if at all possible. Apparently the instinct of going and doing what they normally would in life plays a role in those infected dead that are mobile."

"If you're trying to get away, most highways are gridlocked, so avoid them and any other heavily

traveled roads. Most of southern and northeastern New Jersey has been overrun. I'm sure there are a lot of survivors out there, and hopefully you're listening to us. Sit tight, stay strong, and don't give up. Phone service may be out for the time being, but we're still here. This is Paul Leemin, for WTOK, signing off for today."

"This is impossible." Tony said, nervously. "It's like we're at war or something!"

"What are we gonna do?" Mike asked. "We've got to get out of here."

"Why?" Joe asked. "We're safe here. No one can get in and we've got supplies to hold us over. Do you realize how much she has stored away? Not to mention the generator. The door to get down here from upstairs is solid oak. So even if someone breaks into the house they can't get down here. All we have to do is board up the windows, and there are only two of them."

"You've got a lot of good points there, but I've got to get my wife and kids." Mike said unwavering. "They would know enough to hide out in our own basement, which I set up in case we ever got zapped by another hurricane, but I've got to get to them! I can't leave them alone. What if something happens? I can't even get my wife on the phone!"

"He's right." Tony nodded. "I feel the same way. My wife is alone at the house. My kids are both off in college hours away." He squeezed his eyes shut and shook his head, as if he'd made a decision. "I can't stay here either. I've got to go get them."

"Yeah." Mike said nervously. "I don't think either one of us have a choice."

"You guys are gonna get yourselves killed out there and then you won't be around for anyone!" Joe said.

They heard a crashing sound and ran out of the playroom, stopping dead in their tracks at the sight of Richie.

His skin was pale, grayish in color, and his eyes were downcast, much like the landscapers they fought outside. He still held the whiskey bottle, and acted like he was taking a swig from it even though it was empty.

"Holy shit!" Mike shouted.

Richie looked at him abruptly and started to growl. He charged at Mike who jumped out of the way and knocked him on the floor like a bullfighter.

"This is what they said would happen on the radio." Tony said. "Somebody just give me a fuckin' hammer so I can get this done and over with."

Sam started to cry, then clenched her teeth and turned away as Joe tossed a hammed to Tony.

"Richie, I'm sorry I gotta do this." Tony said, coming up behind him as he snarled and struggled to get to his feet. "I'm not sure you can still hear me in there but I'm sorry."

Without any further hesitation, Tony smashed Richie in the head several times with the hammer. When the body fell and didn't move again, he dropped the hammer on the floor. He covered his face in his hands, wanting to scream and puke at the same time, but he forced himself to do nothing.

TEN

The afternoon was spent in preparation. They all helped to clean up and remove Richie's body.

Joe decided he was going to stay in the basement of the house and Samantha was going to stay with him for the time being. They were going to transfer any useful supplies from upstairs to the basement.

If the basement ever became unsafe or if it looked like they would be overrun they would jump in Joe's jeep, which had been moved into one of the garages, and hightail it to the cabin Sam had inherited.

"We'll be here as long as we can." Joe assured both Tony and Mike. "You guys can get your families and come and stay here if you want. There's more than enough room and it seems rather safe here for the time being."

"I'll keep trying to get through to all of you by phone so if the system is on again at least we'll know where we'll be." Tony said. "I'm going to pick up my wife and we're going to get the kids. If at all possible we'll be back here in a few days."

"I'm going home." Mike said. "We live off the beaten path, so it might be safe enough to stay there. If not, you can bet we'll be here soon."

"I wrote the directions to the cabin out for both of you." Samantha handed them a slip of paper. "If you're stuck and need a place outside of New Jersey, head there."

"We've got all the gas from the landscaper's trucks, and we both know some rural roads to take us home, we should be fine." Mike assured them.

"If worse comes to worse and the roads are too rough to travel," Tony nodded to Mike, "we've both got four-wheel drive trucks, we can go through lawns and fences if we have too."

They said their goodbyes and went their separate ways as the sun went down.

The Beginning

Nick Kisella grew up in Manville, New Jersey, where he began writing fantasy and horror while attending high school. Some of his first published work appeared in the Indie magazines 'Dreadknight', and 'The Nocturnal Lyric'. Since then his work has appeared in various forms from print and online magazines to blogs. His first fantasy novel, 'The Emerald and the Blade' came out in 1989 by a long defunct publisher, with 'The Chalice of Souls' soon to follow. Some of his more recent work includes a screenplay and novelization for 'Nifty Entertainment' a California based

Indie production company, as well as getting the first two fantasy novels he wrote as a teen,'The Chalice of Souls' and 'Death and the Doomweaver' back in print for the sheer nostalgia of it. 'Morningstars', his first full-length horror novel was published by Black Bed Sheet Books in 2012. 'The Beasts and the Walking Dead' a post-apocalyptic fiction novel, has also been published by Black Bed Sheet Books and is the first part of a series. He wrote the novelization to the James Balsamo film, 'I Spill Your Guts', and recently finished the novelization for the Ryan Scott Weber films, 'Mary Horror', and 'Sheriff Tom versus the Zombies'. 'Under Construction' is his second zombie novel taking place before 'The Beasts and the Walking Dead'.

Always having an eventful life, he writes when time allows, usually after dark.

A fitness enthusiast, he has been a certified fitness instructor involved in the industry for twenty years, and continues to stay in shape and train individuals while in his late 40s.

Nick resides in rural Northwestern New Jersey with his wife and twins.

www.ingramcontent.com/pod-product-compliance
Lightning Source LLC
LaVergne TN
LVHW020633100826
845148LV00012B/2172

* 9 7 8 0 6 1 5 9 0 1 8 0 0 *